Sarah, Plain and Tall

Scholastic, Inc., grants teachers permission to photocopy the activity pages from this book for classroom use. No other part of this publication may be reproduced in whole or in part, or stored in a retrieval system, or transmitted in any form or by any means, electronic, mechanical, photocopying, recording, or otherwise, without written permission of the publisher. For information regarding permission, write to Scholastic, Inc., 555 Broadway, New York, NY 10012.

Written by Linda Ward Beech
Cover and interior design by Drew Hires
Interior illustrations by Drew Hires

Photo credits: Cover: SARAH, PLAIN AND TALL by Patricia MacLachlan. Jacket art copyright © 1985 by Marrion Sewall. Jacket copyright © 1985 by Harper Collins Publishers. Reprinted by permission of the Publisher.
Interior: Author photo/John MacLachlan

ISBN 0-590-06572-6
Copyright © 1996 by Scholastic, Inc.
All rights reserved.
Printed in the U.S.A.

Table of Contents

BEFORE READING THE BOOK
Summary 3
Characters 3
About the Author 4
Vocabulary 4
Facts About Fiction 5
What's in an Ad? 5
Getting Started 5

EXPLORING THE BOOK

Chapters 1, 2, and 3
Summary and Discussion Questions 6
Cross-Curricular Activities: Language Arts,
Science, Social Studies 7

Chapters 4, 5, and 6
Summary and Discussion Questions 8
Cross-Curricular Activities: Writing,
Science, Language Arts 9

Chapters 7, 8, and 9
Summary and Discussion Questions 10
Cross-Curricular Activities: Music,
Art, Science 11

SUMMARIZING THE BOOK
Putting It All Together 12
Class, Partner, and Individual Projects 12
Evaluation Ideas 13

STUDENT REPRODUCIBLES
Two Different Places 14
Wanted: A Special Person 15
Gift for a Character 16

Answers for Worksheets 13

Before Reading the Book

SUMMARY

Caleb and Anna live with their father on a farm on the prairie. A sadness has settled over their house since their mother died giving birth to Caleb. One day Papa shows the children a letter from Sarah in Maine in response to an ad he placed for a wife. She says she will come for a month "to see how it is." Sarah comes in the spring bringing along Seal, her cat, and her memories of the sea. The children, Papa, and the animals soon learn to love her. Anna and Caleb worry, though, that she misses the sea too much and will leave them. When Sarah goes to town by herself, they are convinced she has left. However, Sarah returns with gifts for them all and a promise that she will stay.

STORY CHARACTERS

People:

Anna	Caleb's older sister
Caleb	Anna's younger brother
Papa (Jacob Witting)	Father of Anna and Caleb
Sarah	Papa's new wife
William	Sarah's brother
Matthew	Neighbor
Maggie	Matthew's wife
Rose and Violet	Daughters of Matthew and Maggie

Animals:

Lottie and Nick	Family dogs
Jack	Papa's horse
Old Bess	Horse
Seal	Sarah's cat
Harriet, Mattie, Lou	Sheep

ABOUT THE AUTHOR

Patricia MacLachlan admits that when she is driving in a car, she often has conversations with her characters. "I need to have the voices of the characters whisper in my ear," she says.  She attributes her strong sense of fantasy to the many games of make-believe she played with her brothers and sisters while growing up. At the same time the characters in MacLachlan's stories are very real, and her settings are always places that she has been. Patricia MacLachlan was born in Cheyenne, Wyoming, and now lives in the Berkshire Mountains of western Massachusetts. Like many other fine authors, MacLachlan is a passionate reader.

LITERATURE CONNECTIONS
Other Books by Patricia MacLachlan
- *Cassie Binegar*
- *Through Grandpa's Eyes*
- *Unclaimed Treasures*
- *Arthur, for the Very First Time*
- *The Facts and Fictions of Minna Pratt*

SARAH, PLAIN AND TALL was a Newbery Medal winner in 1985. Explain to students that this honor is awarded annually to an author for the most distinguished contribution to American children's literature. As they read the story, ask students to think about why this book was recognized for the Newbery Medal.

VOCABULARY

Students may benefit by working with these vocabulary words. After introducing the list, assign a word to each student. Have students look up their word and present it to the class. You may wish to compile a master list of the words and their definitions on the chalkboard. As a follow-up, challenge students to try one or more of the following activities.

dusk	hearthstone	slab
feisty	rascal	prairie
pesky	shingles	slick
windbreak	flax	paddock
dune	pitchfork	tumbleweed
gullies	killdeer	whickering
squall	pungent	milled
eerie		

- How many of these words can you draw?
- How many of these words name kinds of places?
- How many of these words describe things?

FACTS ABOUT FICTION

Review with students the basic elements of fiction: characters, setting, plot. Point out that in a good story, the characters grow and change in some way as the plot develops. Ask students to choose one of the main characters in *Sarah, Plain and Tall* and note how that character changes from the opening of the story to the end. When you discuss setting, you may wish to use the reproducible on page 14 of this guide.

WHAT'S IN AN AD?

Bring to class some examples of classified advertisements from a local newspaper. Point out that these ads offer things for sale, for rent, and sometimes for trade. Classifieds can also list things that people are looking for such as different kinds of jobs, an apartment to rent, a certain kind of car, or just information. Tell students that in *Sarah, Plain and Tall,* Papa places an ad for a certain kind of person. Before reading the story, have students write down the kind of person they think Papa might be looking for. Is it a farmhand? A tutor for Anna and Caleb? After students discover that Papa is looking for a wife, discuss why he does this by advertising. (*There weren't many single women on the prairie long ago. It was hard to meet new people.*) You may wish to follow-up this discussion with the activity on page 15.

TEACHER TIP

Suggest that students use post-it notes to jot down questions or reactions as they read the story. Students can stick the notes on the relevant pages so they can easily refer to them during a discussion.

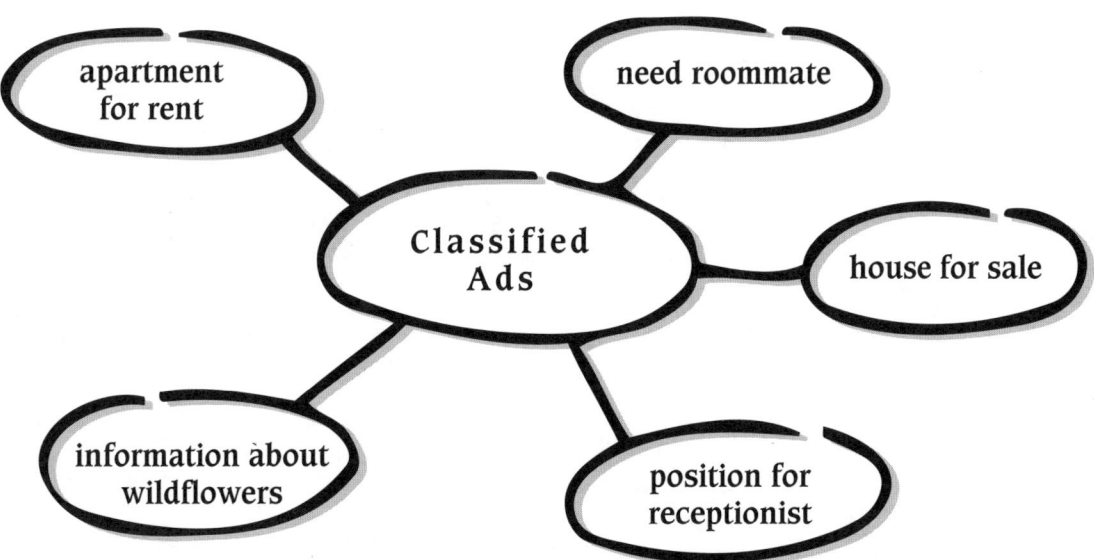

GETTING STARTED

Preview the book before students begin reading it. You might discuss the following:
- *Title* —Who is Sarah? What does it mean when a person is plain?
- *Front Cover*—What can students learn from the picture on the cover? Why are the characters smiling? Why isn't the picture in color?
- *Back Cover*—What questions do students have after reading the blurb?

5

Exploring the Book

CHAPTERS 1, 2, and 3

WHAT HAPPENS

Caleb asks Anna again and again about their Mother who died just after he was born. Both the children miss her greatly. So does their father who "doesn't sing anymore." One night he tells the children that he placed an ad in a newspaper for a wife and has received an answer. It is a letter from Sarah Elisabeth Wheaton who lives in Maine and has a cat. The children and Papa all write to Sarah who carefully replies to each. They are much relieved to learn that she sings. Then in the spring, Sarah arrives with her cat Seal and souvenirs of the Maine seacoast. Almost immediately, Anna and Caleb worry that Sarah will be homesick.

QUESTIONS TO TALK ABOUT

COMPREHENSION AND RECALL

1. What does Anna think is the worst thing about Caleb? (*Mama died after having him.*)

2. Why does Sarah say in her letter that she feels a move is necessary? (*Her brother William is getting married; the new wife is "energetic" and may not want another woman around.*)

HIGHER LEVEL THINKING SKILLS

3. Why do you think Papa has forgotten the old songs? (*They make him sad; remind him of Mama.*)

4. Why does Caleb ask about his mother so much? (*He is trying to connect with her; he never knew her.*)

5. What do you think Anna asked Sarah in her letter? (*Can she braid hair? Can she make stew, bake bread? What are her favorite colors?*)

6. Why does Sarah bring a shell and sea stone from Maine? (*Possible answers: to remind her of the sea; wants to share the sea with Caleb and Anna because she knows they are curious.*)

7. How do you think Sarah feels when she first sees the farm? (*Possible answers: homesick, lonely, challenged, overwhelmed, touched*)

LITERARY ELEMENTS

8. Sarah says she is not mild-mannered. What are some examples to support this? (*She makes up her own mind about things; she is blunt; she prefers building bookcases to making stew.*)

PERSONAL RESPONSE

9. When you read Sarah's letters, how do you feel about her? Why? (*Answers will vary.*)

CROSS-CURRICULAR ACTIVITIES

LANGUAGE ARTS: *Two Words*
Remind students of the book's title, *Sarah, Plain and Tall.* Point out that Sarah uses these two words to describe herself in her letter to Papa. Have students work with a partner. First, each student should write down two words that they think best describe themselves. Then students should share and discuss these words with their partners. If desired, students can then revise their words. When each student has settled on a final two words, pass out index cards. Have students write their words on a card. Post the cards on a bulletin board and take turns reading each set aloud. Can the rest of the class guess who the two words describe?

SCIENCE: *Seeing Sea Birds*
In the story Sarah sends a book of sea birds to Anna. Interested students might do research to learn the names of some of the birds Sarah saw along the coast of Maine. Students might put together mini books with their own illustrations of these birds.

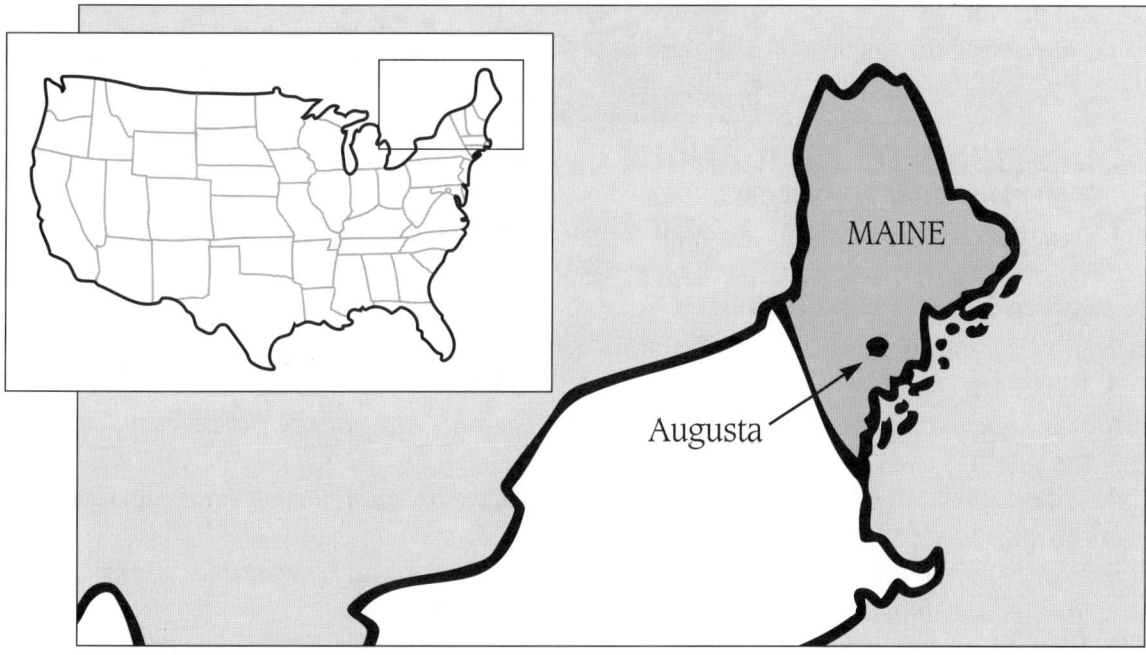

SOCIAL STUDIES: *Maine on the Map*
Display a map of the United States and help students locate Maine. Have a volunteer trace its long, jagged coastline and point out its many islands. Explain that Maine has about 2,000 islands which were formed by a glacier that melted and sank much of the land on the coast. The islands are the peaks of mountains which are now submerged. Then pose the following questions:
- In what part of the United States is Maine? (*northeast*)
- What is the capital of Maine? (*Augusta*)
- Why do you think Maine is a popular summer vacation destination? (*Its many islands and coastline make it enjoyable for swimming and boating. It is also very beautiful.*)

CHAPTERS 4, 5, and 6

WHAT HAPPENS

Sarah quickly wins the hearts of the family and its pets. The children constantly look for signs that she will stay. Sarah not only sings, but she shares her delight with flowers, animals, and even the cow pond. She refers often to the sea that she has left behind. When she talks about sand dunes, Papa shows her the hay mound and calls it "Our dune." Sarah also draws pictures, but the one of the fields is missing something.

QUESTIONS TO TALK ABOUT

COMPREHENSION AND RECALL

1. How do you know that it was hard for Sarah to leave Maine? (*She talks about it often; sends letters and pictures home.*)

HIGHER LEVEL THINKING SKILLS

2. Why do you think the dogs love Sarah? (*She loves animals; they can tell.*)
3. How does Papa feel about Sarah? How do you know? (*He likes her and does things to please her—compliments her stew; tosses his hair for the birds; learns Sarah's song.*)
4. Why does Sarah draw pictures to send home? (*She probably doesn't have a camera; wants to share her new experiences with William.*)
5. Why is Sarah quiet when Papa shows her the "dune" of hay? (*Possible: she is surprised; she understands that he wants her to be happy.*)
6. Why does Sarah ask about winter? (*She realizes she will have to decide about staying before that; winter on the prairie could be very lonely.*)
7. Why do Caleb and Anna love Sarah? (*She is kind, gentle, straightforward, fun to be with. She cares for them.*)

LITERARY ELEMENTS

8. How does the author describe the prairie? (*She mentions many flowers, birds, and animals. She describes the insects buzzing, rustle of cows in grasses, meadows, wind, fields rolling like the sea.*)

PERSONAL RESPONSE

9. Have you ever been homesick? Can you explain how Sarah feels? (*Answers will vary.*)

CROSS-CURRICULAR ACTIVITIES

WRITING: *Dear William*
Remind students that Sarah lived with her brother for many years. Ask them to pretend that they are Sarah and are writing to William to describe life on the prairie farm with Anna, Caleb, and Papa. Students might also wish to illustrate their letters. Have volunteers share the finished letters, then display them on a classroom wall.

SCIENCE: *Wildflower Posters*
Compile a list of the wildflowers mentioned in the story—paintbrush, clover, prairie violets, bride's bonnet, goldenrod, wild asters, woolly ragwort. Discuss how wildflowers add to the environment. Be sure to tell students that many wildflowers are endangered and should not be picked. Invite students to learn the names of wildflowers in your region and to create posters informing people about them. Display the wildflower posters in a school hallway.

LANGUAGE ARTS: *Ways to Say "Yes"*
Remind students that Sarah, like many people from Maine, says, "Ayuh" for "yes." How many other ways can students think of to say "yes"? For example: *sure, okay, yep, right.* Challenge students to make a list of ways to say "yes." How many other languages can they say "yes" in?

CHAPTERS 7, 8, and 9

WHAT HAPPENS

The neighbors Matthew and Maggie come to help plow a field for corn. Maggie understands how Sarah feels and brings her flowers for a garden. She also brings Sarah some chickens for eating, but Anna wisely realizes that Sarah will never eat them. Sarah helps Papa fix the roof, and when a storm comes, the roof holds up well. Sarah gets Papa to teach her how to drive the wagon, and then she goes to town by herself. Anna and Caleb wait anxiously for her return. When she finally appears, she has brought gifts, including three colored pencils for her drawing of the sea. Sarah plans to stay and marry Papa.

QUESTIONS TO TALK ABOUT

COMPREHENSION AND RECALL

1. How does Anna know that the chickens would not be for eating? (*She knows that Sarah loves animals.*)

2. What are some of the ways that Sarah brings the sea to the prairie? (*She talks about it; draws it; buys colored pencils to color it.*)

HIGHER LEVEL THINKING SKILLS

3. Why do you think Maggie knows that Sarah is lonely? (*She too was a mail order bride. She came from Tennessee to the prairie.*)

4. Why does Sarah walk for a long time after the wagon when Maggie and her family leave? (*She feels close to Maggie. Maggie understands what it is like to come a long way from home and join a new family.*)

5. Why does Sarah want to learn how to drive the wagon and go to town? (*She wants some independence; she is her own person.*)

6. How do you know that the animals are afraid in the storm? (*Nick creeps under Anna's arm; Mattie stands close. Seal gets on Anna's lap.*)

7. Why are Sarah's shells at the bottom of the bag of food the family eats in the barn during the storm? (*Possible answers: They are important to her—people take precious things with them when they flee for safety.*)

8. Why does Caleb think that Sarah will not come back when she goes to town? (*He is afraid of losing her.*)

LITERARY ELEMENTS

9. When Sarah returns, how does the author show that Caleb is a little boy? (*He says that Seal was worried because he doesn't want Sarah to know how worried he was that she wouldn't return. Then he cries and says the house is too small and he is loud and pesky.*)

PERSONAL RESPONSE

10. What part of the story did you like the best? Why?

11. Why does Sarah say she is "plain and tall"? Do you think this is a good description of her? How would you describe her? (*Possible answers: She thinks of herself that way because she is an honest, straightforward person. These are admirable qualities in her mind.*)

CROSS-CURRICULAR ACTIVITIES

MUSIC: *We Sing*

Point out to students that long ago, families often sang together for recreation and entertainment. Ask students to give reasons why people did this. (*There were far fewer forms of entertainment then—no radio, television, movies, videos, computer games, CD players.*) Invite students to make a class collection of favorite songs. These can include old favorites as well as contemporary songs. Set aside time during the week for the class to sing together.

ART: *Colors of the Sea*

Sarah describes the sea near Maine as blue, gray, and green. Suggest that students find reproductions of sea paintings done by famous artists such as Winslow Homer. Display the paintings and discuss the colors these artists used to paint the sea. Then challenge students to select three colors to show an environment that is special to them.

SCIENCE: *Birds Building*

On the last page of the book, Anna mentions that "there will be nests of curls to look for." Help students recall the earlier scene where Sarah cuts Caleb's and Papa's hair and says that the birds will use it to build nests. Then invite students to help the birds in your community find building materials. Collect pieces of net, bits of ribbon, cotton, string, hair cuttings, down, tiny twigs, and other similar materials. Make small pouches from the net and fill them with the building materials. Hang the pouches on a tree where birds can find them in the early spring. Students will be amazed at the different materials birds use and the variety of nests they build.

Summarizing the Book

PUTTING IT ALL TOGETHER
You can choose from the following activities as a way to help students summarize and appreciate *Sarah, Plain and Tall*.

CLASS PROJECT: *Character Collages*
Have students work in groups. Assign each group a character from the story. The groups should then meet to discuss their character and brainstorm ways of portraying him or her in a collage. For example, students might list a character's possessions, interests, words, and qualities. Then have students collect materials to use in their collages. Provide each group with a large sheet of oak tag, glue, and scissors. Suggest that the groups divide tasks into 1) designing or sketching the collage; 2) executing the design; 3) writing an explanation. Have the different groups present their character collages to the class, then display them all together to summarize the story.

PARTNER PROJECT: *Our Awards*
Ask each team to think of a special award to give the four main characters in the story—Anna, Caleb, Sarah, and Papa. Explain that the awards should reflect something about the character. For example Papa might be given an award for his good idea (advertising for a wife). Students should be prepared to defend their awards when they present them to the class.

INDIVIDUAL PROJECT: *Colorful Covers*
Discuss the book's cover. Ask: Why do you think the illustrator chose this scene to portray? Then challenge students to design their own covers for *Sarah, Plain and Tall*. Suggest that they use color in their designs. Use the covers to create a display on a class bulletin board.

INDIVIDUAL PROJECT: *Book Mobiles*
As a way to review the story, you might have students make mobiles from wire hangers and other items of their choice. Tell students they should be able to explain

the significance of each item they include. For example, if a student includes a cat or picture of a cat, he or she should explain that the cat is Seal, Sarah's cat from Maine. After students present their book mobiles to the class, hang them from the ceiling.

EVALUATION IDEAS

Students can participate in assessing their work by helping to create a rubric for the project(s) they work on. A sample rubric for the Book Mobile might include the following questions:
• Did the student demonstrate a good understanding of the story by the items included?
• Did the student show originality in the choice of objects?
• Did the student explain the significance of each item well?
• Did the student show good preparation and care in executing the mobile?

Possible Answers for Worksheet

page 14: Maine coast—seals, scallop, oyster, gull, sand dune; Both—wind, squalls; Prairie—hay, meadowlark, tumbleweed, cow pond, gopher
page 15: Students' ads will vary, but should include some specific requirements.
page 16: Students' gifts will vary, but should demonstrate an understanding of the character.

Name: _____

Two Different Places

In the story Sarah comes to live on the prairie. However, she often talks about the seacoast of Maine. How do her two homes differ? How are they alike? Write the words below in the diagram under the correct heading.

hay	wind	tumbleweed
gopher	oyster	sand dune
squalls	gull	cow pond
meadowlark	scallop	seals

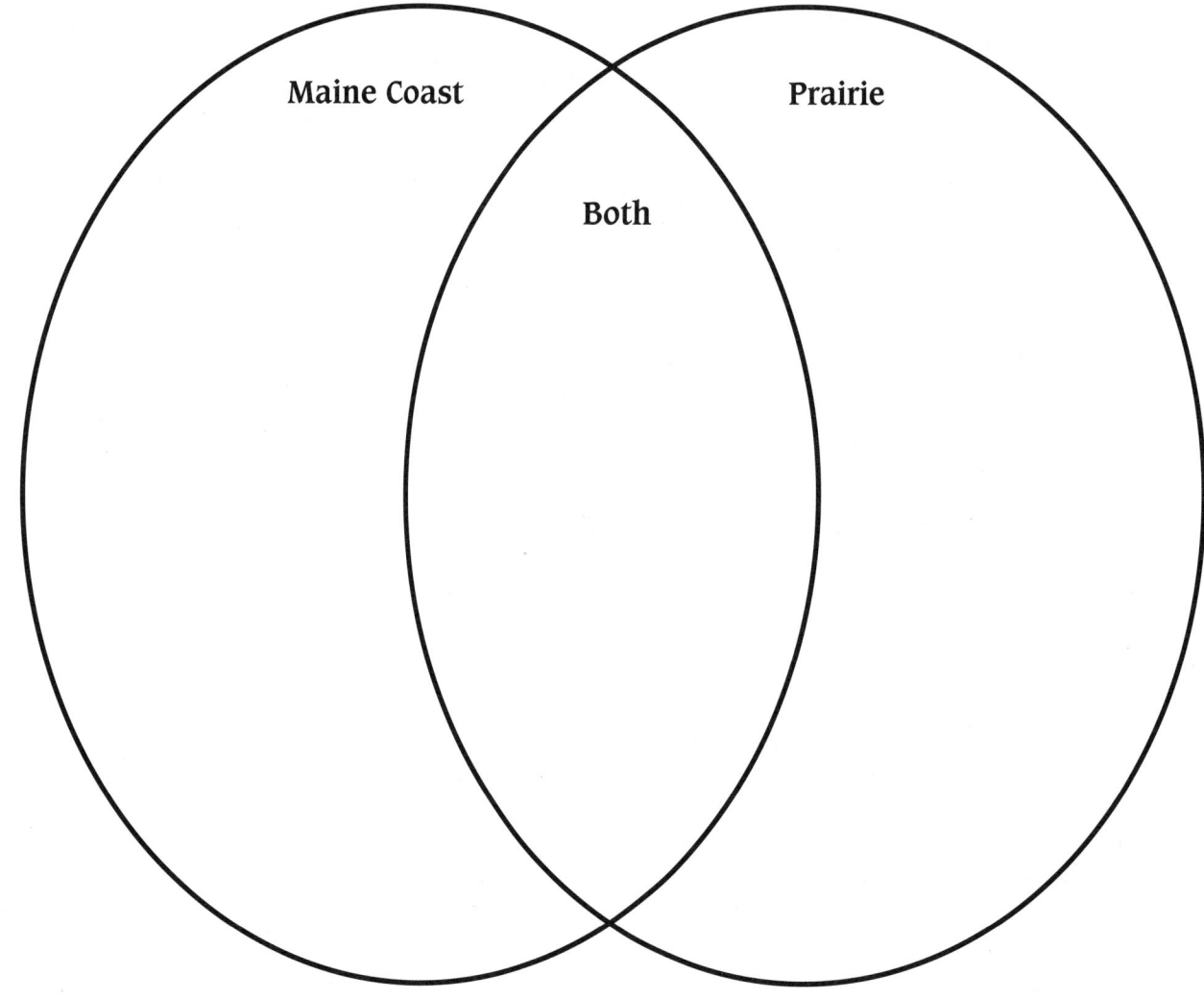

14

Name: _____

Wanted: A Special Person

Papa puts an ad in the newspaper for a wife. What do you suppose he said in this ad?
Think of a special person you would like to have in your life. Perhaps this person will be a new friend, a teacher, or a family member. Write an ad for this person. Include these things:

1. The role this person will have in your life.
2. Some characteristics that this person should have.
3. Some talents or other abilities that this person should have.
4. What you can offer this person.

Daily News
Classified Advertisements

Wanted: _____

Name: _____

Gift for a Character

Who is your favorite character in the story? Think of what you know about this character. Then decide on a gift that you would like to give him or her. Draw a picture of this gift. Then write a paragraph about why you chose it.

Character: _____